The Legend of The Goose Girl

By
Rupert Procter

Inspired by Mia Procter and dedicated to

everyone out there who likes a good old fashioned yarn

Contents

The beginning

Some people say, 'She still lives in the wood.'

Well, I've tried to find her but I never could.

Where is she now?

God alone knows, but I know the story and

here is how it goes.

Once upon a time, a long, long time ago, when the peaks were still covered by ice and snow; and dragons and monsters roamed the land, chased by St George, spear in hand.

A time when evil people did evil things to beautiful princesses, who had to be rescued by magical kings. Yes, it was during these times of famine, war and strife, that a child named Khalia, entered this life.

Her parents, Karl and Nadia were peasants. They gave her that name, which was fitting and right because Khalia means 'most beautiful light'.

She was a happy little baby, really sweet and before long she was on her little feet. However, when Khalia was four, her father was sent to fight in the war and never returned.

Nadia cried and cried for him every day because she was so sad and so was Khalia, because she had lost her dad.

Her poor mother's heart was broken, she went mad. Nadia lost the home and couldn't look after Khalia anymore, all of this because of a stupid, pointless war.

Legend says that Khalia never spoke to the villagers again and howled like a wolf at the moon to let out her pain.

The villagers asked the clergyman, 'What's to be done?' He said, 'Cast her out, she's weird, an evil one; folk like her should be afeared.'

So the villagers cast her out of the village, using sticks and bricks and stones; and told her that if she dared come back, they would break her bones. Now, all of this is important information and needs to be understood because that is how Khalia came to live in the wood.

Khalia made her home amongst the trees,
fashioned out of branches, twigs, mud and moss;
bracken and leaves. Her friends were the deer,
badgers, foxes; hedgehogs, rabbits and the like
and her best friend was a little mouse that she
called Mike, who she endlessly talked to with
kisses and squeaks; Khalia must have been
very clever because she was fluent in 'mouse'
in a couple of weeks.

12

In the spring and summer, they gathered and ate the corn and berries; nuts and occasionally cherries, all gathered from around the wood.

Khalia also hid lots of nuts and corn away for the winter, because the squirrels had told her that she should.

However, despite the best efforts of her friends, life was sometimes hard and Khalia felt sad because she missed her mum and kept thinking about her dad, wanting him to come home so that her mum would no longer be mad.

All these thoughts and feelings were difficult to deal with, which was rotten luck because Khalia was not to blame; yet, with all this sadness she was really stuck.

Khalia wept a little and then the badger enquired, 'What are you going to do?'
When all of a sudden, my goodness, out of the blue; a cacophony of sound as yet unheard, definitely not man; possibly bird?

The bad spell was broken and Khalia jumped to
her feet and ran to the edge of the wood to see
who it was that sang so sweet; when she got there,
she could hardly believe her eyes.

There were hundreds of geese descending from the skies, one after another; they twisted and turned and tumbled down, until each and every one of them was safely on the ground. They totalled in number 282, which meant Khalia now had plenty of befriending to do.

Narugander

*The head of the geese was called Narugander.
He was much bigger than the others and walked
around with an air of great grandeur. Khalia could
tell that Narugander was the leader as soon as he
spoke, because there was a great deal of honking
and then nobody spoke for quite some time, while
they all got out of a 'V' and stood in a line. I mean,
it wasn't exactly a line, it was more like a sort of
crowded mess; apparently they call it a gaggle;
that's G.A.GG.L.E for gaggle, anyway, sorry I digress.*

Narugander flapped his wings and rose to his feet, honking and honking with all his might.

Khalia couldn't understand exactly what he said, but it was something like 'Is everyone alright?'

Well, of course they weren't; it had been a hell of a flight and they'd had to endure all sorts of things like storms and thunder and lightning. They had even been shot at with pebbles from slings. In fact, some of the geese had injured their wings.

One poor goose by the name Fred was so tired
when Khalia found him she thought he was
dead; luckily he wasn't, he was only sleeping,
which I can assure you, saved a great deal of
weeping because, geese, you see, really care about
each other. It's like everyone's your sister and
everyone's your brother.

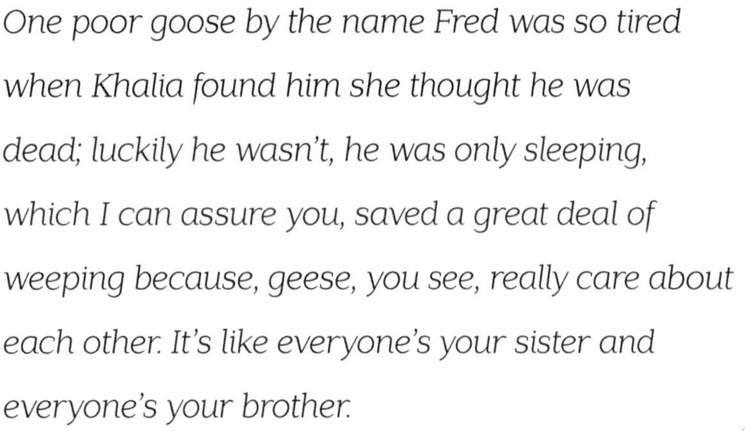

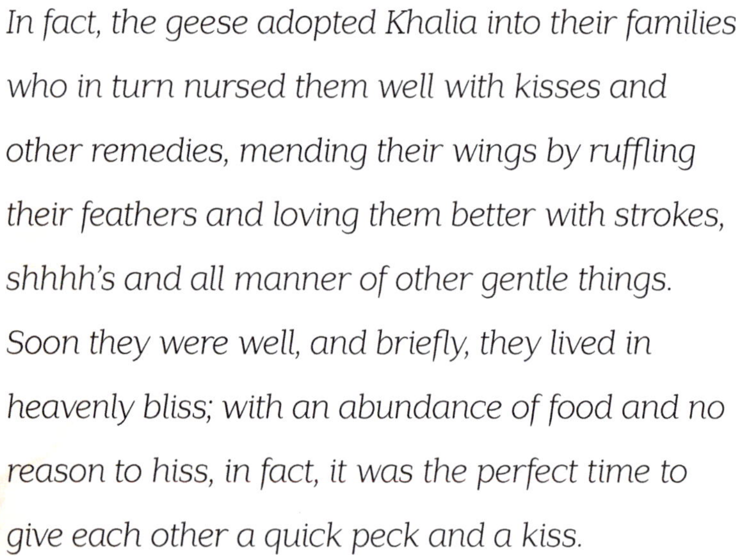

In fact, the geese adopted Khalia into their families
who in turn nursed them well with kisses and
other remedies, mending their wings by ruffling
their feathers and loving them better with strokes,
shhhh's and all manner of other gentle things.
Soon they were well, and briefly, they lived in
heavenly bliss; with an abundance of food and no
reason to hiss, in fact, it was the perfect time to
give each other a quick peck and a kiss.

Count Badomen

Meanwhile in the village, there was trouble brewing. In fact, it wasn't just brewing, it was positively stewing.

For the evil Count Badomen, a despicable man who owned all the land, was putting a gold coin into the hand of a terrible villain, who was also a spy and had been paid by his lordship to 'look out for geese in the sky.'

Well the news he received had Badomen skipping and dancing and legend says even laughing, for only the second time in his life; the first was when he got rid of his wife.

The news was apparently, 'Music to my ears, in fact, I've been waiting to hear this news for years and years,' for the geese, you see, had landed right on his plot.

'Excellent,' he said, 'no man shall rest until we've killed the lot.'

For the evil Count was planning to feast and the only thing on the menu was roasted geese.

His trumpeters blew their trumpets and the
villagers all gathered in a mob, while Badomen
explained he wanted to put a goose in his gob. He
bribed them with 'A reward of five gold pieces, to
the man who catches the five biggest geeses.'

Then they all cheered and clapped whilst he
raised his hand to offer, 'A silver guinea to any
child, woman or man, who makes the noose that
is judged most efficient at killing a goose.' The
mob all cheered again, as mobs do, and that went
on for a minute or two.

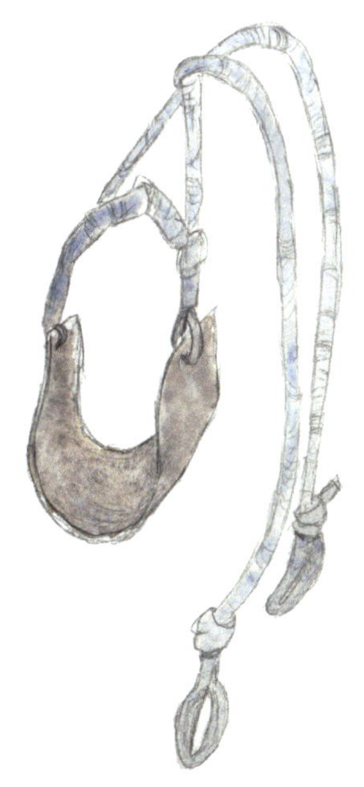

Badomen then ordered the mob to, 'Go to your
homes and busy yourselves making spears
and cudgels, arrows and slings, and other vile
weapons like spikey things, and in particular,
things what's good at breaking wings.'

More clapping and back slapping, before,
'Listen up you lot; most important, and lest ye
forget. You've all got to help make the really big
net.' They all then cackled, because they were
a bloodthirsty bunch and agreed to start the
killing tomorrow, right after lunch.'

The wizard

The next morning, in the wood, a wizard appeared. He had an unusual hat and a long grey beard. He was a funny looking chap, with a very nice nose and wore a great big cloak that went right down to his toes. It was really weird when he walked around, because it looked like he was floating above the ground.

He said his name was Margeeshan, and that he'd come to warn them of the plot of the evil Badomen. He told Khalia not to worry because he knew exactly what to do, but before he could tell her, he desperately needed to use the loo.

When Margeeshan returned, he showed Khalia
lots of tricks; like how to make useful things out of
useless sticks.

Then, and most importantly, he taught her a
magical spell that involved multiplying threes; a
spell to use against evil enemies.

He then lent her a mirror and told her to comb
her hair, but when she looked up from her mirror,
he had vanished into thin air.

28

Now, Margeeshan had also told Khalia a promise to keep. A promise to urgently wake the geese from their sleep and warn them of the plot of Badomen. Well, she didn't waste a moment after he'd vanished but rushed to where they lay, fast asleep amongst the stubbles, in a field of hay.

She told the poor geese, who were of course very alarmed. I mean, they were just geese for God's sake and these men were armed. Even worse, it seemed obvious that what these men wanted to do was to turn the geese into 'goosy' stew.

There was plenty of panic, honking and hissing of course; and a great deal of flapping, which just made everything worse.

The battle

It was no sooner than the noisy panic had really set in, that Khalia was alerted to a very different and worrying type of din. Coming straight towards them, at a very fast pace, was a short fat man on a horse with a big grin on his face. Yes, you've guessed it, Badomen, the world's worst imaginable type of thuggish hooligan; closely followed by his angry mob of bloodthirsty men, whose only thought regarding the geese was to kill every last one of them.

My word, did they make a din, with their sabres a rattling and their armour of tin; the clattering of all those other things they'd made, like cudgels and spears and the spikers and nooses and other vile things for killing gooses; they certainly made a lot of noise, so much so that even Narugander gulped and lost his poise.

Poor little Khalia was totally taken by surprise and could hardly think, when all of a sudden there was an almighty clink and this contraption catapulted this huge net into the air and captured half the geese quicker than a sheep can go Baaaaaaaa!

Badomen then dismounted his horse and pointed his fat finger at Khalia of course and demanded, 'Her capture, dead or alive, but preferably dead'; clearly, a horrible thing to say, that should never have been said. I mean, the man was evil and off his head.

Things were not going at all well when Khalia suddenly remembered the wizards spell, you know the one where she had to multiply threes; the spell that works against your enemies:

'One times three is three and three times three is nine, Margeeshan, Margeeshan, this is rescue time.'

But guess what, nothing happened, not a thing; not even a sprinkling of fairy dust.

Just the renewed twang of someone's sling and the 'whoosh' of another crossbow bolt aimed right at a gooses throat; just the endless sounds of war, sounds that her poor father must have heard before he died. Needless to say, poor Khalia was defeated and just cried and cried. It was at this time that Badomen's lot did the pincer movement by doubling back, which meant that now his Lordship from all sides could attack.

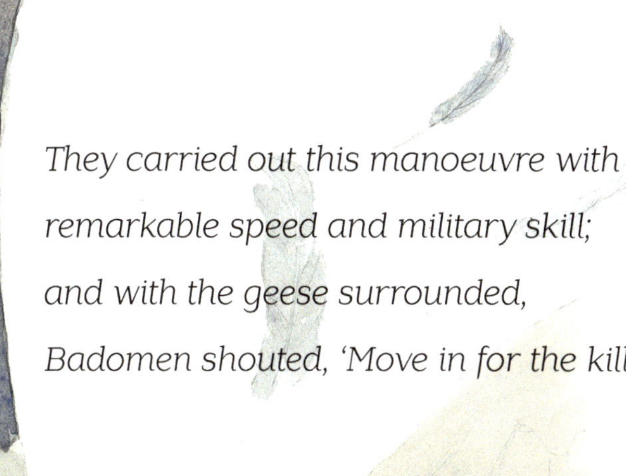

They carried out this manoeuvre with remarkable speed and military skill; and with the geese surrounded, Badomen shouted, 'Move in for the kill.'

The unicorn

Then, all of a sudden, something magical happened; something really good. A unicorn appeared at the edge of the wood, with pricked back ears and sprightly prances and a horn that looked like one of St George's lances. He told Khalia to jump up on his back and be prepared for imminent attack.

He said he had been sent by the wizard, Margeeshan, to kill the evil Badomen. Well, when the villagers saw the unicorn they were filled with fright and told the evil Badomen, 'We've decided not to fight but instead we're heading back home', which of course left Badomen all on his own.

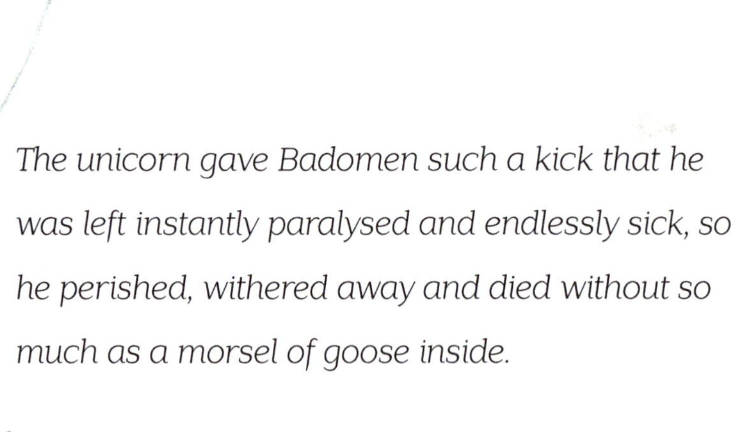

The unicorn gave Badomen such a kick that he was left instantly paralysed and endlessly sick, so he perished, withered away and died without so much as a morsel of goose inside.

It was an unexpected victory but one that was thoroughly deserved; a bit like David versus Goliath, except, this time, David was a bird. The geese celebrated, as they do, by going for a swim. Followed, for some reason, by a rendition of 'God save the king,' which went something like '(Honk, God save the king, a bit)', I'll just honk that bit, I won't do the whole thing.

Anyway, it seemed to do the trick and put everyone in the party mood and before long everyone's thoughts were turning to food.

The flight of the geese

That evening, all the geese gathered in a gaggle on the gentle slopes between the shores of the Emerald Lake and the woods; a place called 'The fairies hill' and the story goes:

'They supped there until they'd had their fill of the grasses, corn and berries; nuts and cherries'. Khalia was guest of honour, along with the wizard, the unicorn and some bloke called Trevor, a conservationist for the RSPB, who had untangled the net and set the birds free; of course, Khalia's friends were invited too.

The deer, the badger and the foxes; the rabbits, hedgehogs and the mice; in fact, everyone nice. They all celebrated and danced because they were delighted, for they had won the day when it looked like they were doomed and yet by some miracle normal life had resumed.

They danced the 'wobbly knees' and other such olden dances like the Conga and went skipping, dancing, weaving and prancing through the trees; on pathways made of golden leaves until they could dance no longer and returned to 'The fairies hill', where it seemed for a moment that time stood still as they all gazed and gazed, and gazed at the big moon, the stars and space.

Trevor was so happy he had tears running down

his face, but, to be fair, it was a beautiful sight; the

woods, water, hills and all of that lot bathed in

the moonlight.

It was beautiful because the more they gazed,

the more they were amazed by the beauty of that

sccnc; that serene scene.

The Margeeshan then spoke. He said, 'magic is all

around', which was quite profound, but then again

he was a profound sort of a bloke. The geese were

all then hissing themselves laughing at his joke,

about some poor fellow who had fancied a swim,

but when he got there, was too scared to get in;

and soon he was up to his usual tricks, making
useful things out of useless sticks, including a
couple of odd looking things, that were sort of
sticks and twigs tied together with strings. They
looked a bit like goose wings but without a single
feather. It was an excellent trick and one of his
best; the geese were clearly impressed. He handed
the objects to Khalia, who loved them and started
to cry because her deepest desire was to be
able to fly.

The Margeeshan plaited goose feathers into her hair and the twiggy wing things. In fact, he plaited goose feathers everywhere, and waving his magic staff above his head, legend has it these words were said: 'Tonight, in magic we shall delight, for Khalia means most beautiful light. Khalia, Khalia do not cry, for with the geese you shall fly.' Then, with all his might, he stuck his stick into the ground and there was this rumbling sound, under the ground, all around; it was like a mini earthquake.

Khalia then noticed a curious thing; she noticed
that Narugander had stretched out one great
wing and was pointing directly at the moon,
honking something about 'they must all be leaving
soon and that he had been spoken to earlier by
the sun, who had reminded him that at dawn they
must continue on the long journey that they had
already begun'.

Narugander then addressed Khalia directly in his distinctive voice and in a manner which left her little or no choice, he said: 'Khalia, Khalia, stop your fuss, we're not leaving without you because you are one of us. When we arrived we numbered 282, including me; but when we leave we will number 283'.

Well, with that said, there was a great deal of commotion and a general outpouring of emotion as the geese all honked their approval, raising themselves up by flapping their wings and did all sorts of other excited 'goosy' things.

As dawn approached, there was even further unrest as the geese did their best honking, putting their wings to the test. Then, just as the almighty sun rose, Narugander spoke again:

'The forecast was pretty good but they could expect a little rain. However, today is the day and conditions seem just right; so, follow me and let us, together, all take flight.'

With that, they all rushed down the bank, honking
and flapping in order of rank and one after
another they took to the air, including a little girl
with curly, blond hair.

It was an absolutely unbelievable sight and the first
ever recorded human flight. It was as if she knew
exactly what to do; she just flew, and she really could
fly. She flew up and up and up into the big blue sky;
flapping her wings, fly, fly, fly, flying, up, up, up into
the air, off to a place called Somewhere.

Some people say that Khalia still lives in the wood,

well, I tried to find her but I never could.

Where is she now?

God alone knows, but that's how the story goes.

The end